Grayslake Area Public Library District
Grayslake, Illinois

1. A fine will be charged on each book which is not returned when it is due.

2. All injuries to books beyond reasonable wear and all losses shall be made good to the satisfaction of the Librarian.

3. Each borrower is held responsible for all books drawn on his card and for all fines accruing on the same.

DEMCO

Molly Mouse Is Shy

A Story of Shyness

Published in 2010 by Windmill Books, LLC
303 Park Avenue South Suite # 1280, New York, NY 10010-3657

Adaptations to North American Edition © 2010 Windmill Books

First published in Great Britain in hardback in 2001 by Brimax Publishing Ltd
First paperback edition published in Great Britain in 2002 by Brimax Publishing Ltd
Appledram Barns, Birdham Road, Chichester, PO20 7EQ, UK
© Brimax Publishing Ltd

CREDITS:
Author: Lynne Gibbs, Illustrator: Melanie Mitchell

Library of Congress Cataloging-in-Publication Data

Gibbs, Lynne.
 [Quiet as a mouse]
 Molly Mouse is shy : a story of shyness / text by Lynne Gibbs ; illustrations by Melanie Mitchell. -- North American ed.
      p. cm. -- (Let's grow together)
 "Alphabet Soup."
 Summary: After Molly, a shy mouse, finally lets her sisters persuade her to go to a party with them, she surprises herself by having a wonderful time.
 ISBN 978-1-60754-756-3 (library binding) -- ISBN 978-1-60754-761-7 (pbk. binding) -- ISBN 978-1-60754-762-4 (6-pack)
 [1. Bashfulness--Fiction. 2. Self-confidence--Fiction. 3. Parties--Fiction. 4. Sisters--Fiction. 5. Mice--Fiction.] I. Mitchell, Melanie, ill. II. Title.
 PZ7.G33922Mol 2010
 [E]--dc22
          2009035882

          3 6109 00357 5609

Manufactured in China

CPSIA Compliance Information: Batch #PW01W: For further information contact Windmill Books, New York, New York at 1-866-478-0556.

Let's Grow Together

Molly Mouse Is Shy
A Story of Shyness

Text by Lynne Gibbs
Illustrations by Melanie Mitchell

alphabet soup™
an imprint of
WINDMILL BOOKS™
New York

It was a very exciting morning in the Mouse House
when three little envelopes plopped onto the doormat.
"A party!" cried Holly and Polly, tearing open
their invitations. "We'll all have a great time."
But Molly did not agree with her sisters. She was so
shy that she blushed if another mouse so much
as twitched his whiskers at her.
"I can't possibly go!" she squeaked.

"You poor thing," said Holly, when she saw Molly.
Her whole face was covered in big, red spots.
"Are you sick?" asked Polly.
"I really don't think that I should go to the
party now," said Molly weakly.
"Oh, you'll be fine," said Mother.
"As long as you wash those spots off first."
She smiled and picked up the red crayon that
Molly had used to draw on the spots.

While her sisters got ready for the party,
Molly desperately tried to think of another plan.
She decided to hide where nobody could find her.
Crawling under her bed, Molly curled up into a tiny ball.
"Molly, where are you?" called her sisters.
She held her breath and kept very, very still.

It was very dusty underneath Molly's
bed and a piece of fluff tickled her nose.
Soon, she could not hold back any longer.
"Achoo!" she sneezed loudly.
"ACHOO! ACHOO! ACHOO!"

"We know where you are," said Holly and Polly
as they peeked under the bed.
"What are you doing?" they asked, giggling.
Feeling silly, Molly crawled out from under her
bed. There must be something else she could do!

"Hurry up, Molly," said Mother, when she saw
her sitting on her bed. "It's almost time for the party."
Molly just sat there, looking forlorn.
"What's the matter?" asked Mother.
Molly held up a piece of paper. It read, "I can't
possibly go to the party. I have lost my squeak."
"Oh dear," tutted Mother. "That is a shame.
I'll go and get some medicine for you."

"Poor you," said Holly, hiding a smile.

"Mother's medicine tastes really horrible."

"I'm glad I don't have to take it," said Polly.

"We're going to have so much fun at the party."

Molly thought for a little while.

Then she gave a little cough and whispered,

"Actually, I think my squeak has just come back.

Maybe I will go to the party after all."

"Don't worry, we'll stay with you the whole time,"

said her sisters.

When they arrived at the party, Molly, Holly, and Polly were soon surrounded by lots of other little mice. "Remember what you promised," Molly squeaked, feeling her cheeks getting redder and redder and hotter and hotter. "Please don't leave me on my own."

"We promise," said Holly and Polly.

"Oh, I wish I was at home," Molly whispered.

Music began to play and the fun began. Molly was soon caught up in a group of dancing mice. "Oh, no!" she gasped.

Molly looked around nervously for her sisters, but soon her feet began to move to the music. Around and around she whirled and twirled with the other mice.

"Where is she?" asked Holly, nervously.

Just then, Molly danced past her sisters. "This party is fun!" she called. "Why don't you two join in?"

Forgetting about being shy, Molly
soon made lots of new friends.

"I can't believe that this is our shy little sister,"
said Polly proudly, as Molly joined in
a game of blindman's bluff.
Wearing a blindfold, Molly searched for the
other mice, bumping into things as she went.
"Got you!" she cried, finding someone
hiding behind a tree.

"Let's play another game!" suggested Molly.
"What shall we play?" asked her new friends.
Molly thought for a while, then exclaimed,
"I know! How about musical chairs?"
The little mice ran around and around a row of chairs.

24

When the music stopped, Molly rushed to find a seat but ended up sitting on the ground! "Whoops!" she said with a giggle.

When it was time to leave, Molly was sad to go.
"I wish we could stay longer," she said with a sigh.
"There will be other parties," Polly assured her.
"I must say goodbye to everyone,"
said Molly, rushing back.

Polly and Holly had to lead Molly from the party.
"Bye, everyone!" called Molly.
"See you again soon."

Back home, Molly told Mother all about the
wonderful time they had had at the party.
"We danced and played games and made lots
of new friends," she reported enthusiastically.
"I knew that you would enjoy it," said Mother.
"Molly was the life of the party," said Holly and Polly.
"I had so much fun," said Molly,
"I'm not so shy after all."

LEARN MORE!

Molly is a pretend mouse. Here are some fun facts so you can learn more about real mice.

- Mice like to eat 10-20 times a day, and even build their homes close to their food source.
- Did you know that mice are nocturnal animals? That means they are active mostly at night.
- Mice have very poor eyesight, and do not see things in color like humans. But they do have an excellent sense of hearing and a great sense of smell.
- People in China first wrote about keeping mice as pets in a book dating back to 1100 BC. That's over 3,000 years ago!
- Did you know that female mice can have babies 8-10 times a year and start giving birth when they are only 2 months old?

For More Information

This story is about a mouse who is shy. Check out the books and Web sites below to learn more about mice or what you can do if you are feeling like Molly!

Books

Brozovich, Richard and Linda Chase. Say goodbye to being shy: A workbook to help kids overcome shyness. Oakland, CA: Instant Help Books, 2008.

Jackson, J.S. and R.W. Alley. Shyness isn't a minus: How to turn bashfulness into a plus. St. Meinrad, IN: One Caring Place, 2006.

Johnson, Jinny. Rats and mice (Get to know your pet). Saunders Book Co, 2009.

Roca, Nuria. Are you shy? (Let's talk about it books). Hauppauge, NY: Barron's Educational Series, 2006.

Savage, Stephen. Mouse (Animal neighbors). New York: Rosen Publishing, 2008.

Web Sites

To ensure the currency and safety of recommended Internet links, Windmill maintains and updates an online list of sites related to the subject of this book. To access this list of Web sites, please go to www.windmillbooks.com/weblinks and select this book's title.

For more great fiction and nonfiction, go to
www.windmillbooks.com.